Audrey and Barbara

written and illustrated

by

Janet Lawson

POCKET
BOOKS

London · New York · Sydney

For Phil, my best friend and fellow adventurer

POCKET
BOOKS

First published in Great Britain in 2002 by Simon & Schuster UK Ltd,
Africa House, 64-78 Kingsway, London WC2B 6AH.

This edition published in 2003 by Pocket Books,
an imprint of Simon & Schuster UK Ltd
Originally published in the USA by
Simon & Schuster Children's Books in 2002

Text Copyright © 2002 by Janet Lawson.
Illustration Copyright © 2002 by Janet Lawson.
Book design by Kristin Smith.
The text of this book is set in Truesdell.
The illustrations are rendered in watercolour.

ISBN 07434 6214 9

Printed in China

1 3 5 7 9 10 8 6 4 2

"Barbara," asked Audrey, "how would you like to ride an elephant?"

"Will I have to get off my pillow?"

"Yes. We need to go to India. It's time for an adventure."

"What about my nap?" asked Barbara.
"You can nap after we see the Taj Mahal."

"If I were to go to India," asked Barbara, "why would I want
  to see the Taj Mahal?"

"Because it's beautiful."

"My pillow is beautiful. Let's go back inside and see it."

"No," said Audrey. "We have a long way to go. India is on
   the other side of the world."
"But what about the ocean?" asked Barbara.
"What ocean?"

"That one," said Barbara. "It's between us and India."
"Oh," said Audrey.

"Looks like I'll have lots of time for a nap."
"Hmmm," said Audrey.

"Where are you going?" asked Barbara.
"I'm looking for turbans."
"Will they get us across the ocean?"

"No, we'll wear them on our heads
    when we ride elephants to the Taj Mahal."
"What about the ocean?" asked Barbara.

"We're going to swim across it."

"Not me," said Barbara.

"Why not?"

"I don't like to get wet."

"Oh," said Audrey.

"What are you doing?" asked Barbara.

"I'm thinking."

"It looks a lot like napping. Should I get my pillow?"

"No. We're going to build a boat."

"When we get to India," Audrey said, "we'll see a snake charmer."

"What's a snake charmer?"
"A person who plays a horn until a poisonous snake
    dances out of a basket."

"Will it bite me?" asked Barbara.

"Not if we bow properly to the charmer. Then he will protect us."

"We're ready to sail," said Audrey.

"It's a nice boat," said Barbara. "But how will we get it to the ocean?"

"It's not moving," said Barbara.

"I know."

"Where are you going now?" asked Barbara.
"To the garage. I know just what we need."

"We can use this," said Audrey. "Things always work out
   when you decide to go on an adventure."
"Are you talking about this adventure?" asked Barbara.
"Of course."

"Are you going to build another boat?" asked Barbara.

"No. I'm going to roll this one out of the bathroom."

"If we hurry," said Audrey, "we'll catch the
      westerly winds. They'll blow us all the way to India."
"What if they stop blowing?" asked Barbara.
"We'll row."

"What if we get tired of rowing?"

"We'll be stuck in the middle of the ocean," said Audrey.

"We could ask a whale for a tow," suggested Barbara.
"That's a great idea," said Audrey.

"Where are you going?" asked Barbara. "India is this way."
"We almost forgot something."

"You think of everything," said Barbara.
"That's how you get to India," said Audrey.

"Are all your adventures this much fun?"
asked Barbara.

"Only the ones with you."